Niles and Bradford

Baseball Bully

By: Marcy Blesy

This book is a work of fiction. Names, characters, places, and events are a result of the imagination of the author or are used fictitiously. Any resemblance to actual persons, living or dead, businesses, events, or locations is a coincidence.

No part of the text may be reproduced without the written permission of the author, except for brief passages in reviews.

Cover design by Cormar Covers

Follow my blog for information about upcoming books or short stories.

Chapter 1:

Being the new kid is not easy. *You will be fine. You are a nice boy,* said his mom. *You will make lots of friends.* But Niles is not so sure about that. There are only two things that Niles feels like he can count on. One thing he knows is that he can play sports. He works hard. Sometimes the hard work pays off, and he does well. He scores a goal. He makes a basket. He gets a hole in one. Sometimes he works hard and doesn't do well, but he likes playing either way.

The other thing Niles can count on is his best friend Bradford. Bradford is Niles's pet dragon. Bradford is not an imaginary friend. He's very much a real, orange, foot tall dragon. He is so good at staying hidden that no one has seen him except for Niles. That includes Niles's mom and dad and big sister Nora. There have been close calls—like the one time that Nora sleepwalked into Niles's room when he and Bradford were playing a late-night poker game. Bradford was teaching Niles how to play the card game. He wasn't a very good teacher, though. They were playing for money, and Niles had already lost $1.87 to Bradford that night. Then Nora walked into Niles's bedroom. She thought she was in the bathroom. No one saw her. Bradford was jumping up and down. He laid down his cards and yelled *full house!* That's three cards of the same kind and two cards of the same kind. That's a really good set of cards to have in poker.

Nora rubbed her eyes and seemed to wake up. She said, *What's that?* Then Bradford went *poof* like he does when he disappears. It's like a cool magic trick. One minute he is there. The next minute he is gone. But it does not last for long before he appears again. Niles got up super quick. He put his hand on Nora's back and pushed her gently toward the hallway that would lead to the bathroom. *You're dreaming, Nora. Night. Night.* There would be other close calls with Bradford. But so far, he's Niles's special secret.

No, being the new kid is not always easy. But it's summer. Niles will have a chance to make friends before school starts in the fall. It's baseball season. And being on a baseball team with ten other boys is like being dropped into an instant

group of best friends. Niles is ready.

Chapter 2:

The tryouts for the Clearview Dry-Cleaners is not really a tryout at all. Everyone makes the team. All the uniforms are paid for by a business in town. Only the Clearview Dry Cleaners needs more players. So, that is Niles's team.

The coach is a big guy. He doesn't look like he plays a lot of sports now.

"Welcome, boys. My name is Coach Fartzer. You can just call me Coach if you want to."

"I like *Fartzer* better." A tall boy with lots of freckles talks into his baseball glove, but everyone can hear him. A couple of other boys laugh.

"That's enough, Tad. You're nine now. Bathroom jokes are for babies," says Coach.

"Yes, Coach Fartzer," says Tad.

Nobody else laughs this time. Everyone knows this Tad guy likes to make trouble.

"Boys, we are going to start with some warm-ups. Run from home plate to the right field fence and back. Then grab your gloves."

The boys drop any equipment they are holding: bats, balls, gloves, helmets. They run toward the fence. Bradford, who has been listening from Niles's bat bag is getting bored. And hot. Even though he is a dragon, he does not like to sweat. He jumps out of the bag and starts sniffing around. Some of the bags are very fancy. Some have three bats! Niles's bag only has one bat. You can only use one bat at a time anyway. Bradford knocks out a few bats when he's jumping from bag to bag. He doesn't do it on purpose. He just doesn't care. When he gets to the red bag, he stops. Red is Bradford's most favorite color in the whole world. He is like a bull who is attracted to the color red in a bull fight. He can't stay away. Bradford jumps into the side pocket of the red bag. He sniffs around. *Peanut butter. This kid is a-m-a-z-i-n-g!* thinks Bradford. He gobbles up the peanut butter sandwich but throws out the crusts. Niles always cuts off the crusts when he makes Bradford's sandwich. Plus, no jelly—ever.

The sound of pounding feet alerts Bradford. The boys are back.

"Grab your gloves," says Coach. "Find a partner. Play some catch. Nothing crazy, just nice easy throws. We need to warm up those arms."

"Hey! Who ate my peanut butter sandwich?" yells Tad. He points to the ground where pieces of bread crust sit. The ants have found them, too.

"Not me."

"Not me."

"Not me."

"Not me."

No one admits to eating the sandwich. Niles knows. He always knows. Bradford loves peanut butter sandwiches. And peanut butter sandwiches from red bags are even more evidence that

Bradford ate the sandwich. When Niles reaches in his own bag, he feels the tail of Bradford. He sighs with relief. At least he made it back to safety before that bully Tad found him. Bradford needs a strong warning. Stay away from baseball practice!

Chapter 3:

The first game of the baseball season starts in fifteen minutes. Niles is excited. His parents are excited, too. Bradford has been told to stay home. Niles does not want to risk any trouble for his first game. He is still the new kid.

"Okay, boys. Tonight is our first test. How well can we play together? How much have we learned? Let's remember to have some fun, too."

"Who is pitching?" asks Scotty. Scotty asks a lot of questions at practice.

"This is our first game. The coaches are going to pitch. Kyle is going to study the position. He will pitch in a few games later in the season."

"I bet the other team wishes they had a Coach *Fartzer* pitching to them!" says Tad.

Coach stares at Tad. I imagine him shooting lasers with his big brown eyes. But Tad does not even blink.

"Nick, first base! Luke—shortstop, Connor—third base! Otis—catcher! Scotty, Vinnie, and Sammy—split up in the outfield!"

A hand raises.

"Yes, Scotty?"

"Coach, does it matter which outfield spot?"

"Yes, sure. Vinnie—centerfield, Sammy—left field, Scotty—right field."

"Great, thanks," says Scotty. "Is…is right field behind first base or third base?"

"First base, Scotty. We have gone over this before," says Coach.

"Sorry, Coach. Should I go out there now?"

Coach sighs. "Yes, Scotty."

"Niles, grab your glove. You're playing second base."

Niles is surprised but happy. He was hoping to just get in the game, but to play a base will be extra fun.

"Hey!"

It's Tad.

"I play second base not this bony new kid."

"Not today you don't," says Coach Fartzer.

"You're picking on me because you can't take a silly joke about your name," he says.

The coach's face is getting red. "No, I am choosing Niles to play second base because he catches balls and understands how to tag out players."

"Let's go, coaches!" The umpire in the bright blue shirt yells at the coaches of the Clearview Dry Cleaners and The Bayside Bug Zappers.

"Okay, team. Hands up." The players put their hands up in the air, meeting in the middle. "On the count of three...*One, Two, Three, Goooooo Dry Cleaners!*"

The players run to their positions. Tad stomps back to the dugout with Rashid. Rashid smiles—a lot . He is happy all the time. No one understands why, but even Tad's bad attitude doesn't bother him. They are a good combination in the dugout.

Niles pounds his glove a few times with his fist. He has seen other players do that, too. The first two batters strike out. Their coach pitches right to them. They just can't hit the ball. The next player hits the ball far over Niles's head. He runs backward to try to catch him. The ball isn't his, though. It is Scotty's. But Scotty has not moved from his spot in right field. He has not moved even one blade of grass closer to the ball. Coach Fartzer is mad.

"Scotty! Run, Scotty! You can't stay still. You have to *move* to the ball."

Scotty nods his head like he understands. Then he raises his hand like kids do in class when they have a question for the teacher. People in the bleachers laugh.

Coach Fartzer shakes his head like he can't believe it, either. He calls *timeout* to the umpire. He jogs to right field. "What do you need, Scotty?"

"Do I move *before* the ball is hit or *after*?"

"Huh?" Coach scratches his head even though he is wearing a hat, too. But he puts up a hand to stop Scotty from repeating the question. "You move *after* the ball is hit. Run *to* the ball if it is hit close to you, okay, Scotty?"

Scotty shakes his head *yes*. "Thanks, Coach."

The next batter hits a pop fly straight up in the sky. Niles runs forward and snags the ball with his glove. The crowd cheers. Three outs. The Clearview Dry Cleaners are up to bat.

Niles tries to sit as far away from Tad in the dugout as he can. Tad is chewing on sunflower seeds. He spits them as close to Niles as he can reach. We are batting well. Vinnie is on first base. Sammy is on second. It is Niles's turn to bat. Niles swings and misses at the first ball.

"Let's go, Niles! You can do it!" His sister Nora yells from the bleachers.

The second pitch, Niles hits. But it is foul which is the same thing as getting a strike. The third pitch is wild. Niles knows not to swing at that.

"Let's go, Loser!" Niles knows that was *not* his sister Nora yelling. He guesses that it was Tad.

Bradford also hears Tad. He pops his head out of the side of Niles's bat bag. He knows he is not allowed to be at the game. He was too excited to miss the first game of the season, though! Bradford puts his head back in the bag, but he can still see Tad from the opening that is not zipped.

Bradford has a direct view of Tad's water bottle. He knows he should behave. He knows he came to watch the game, but he can't let his best friend Niles be called names like that, either.

"Stand up and watch the batters," Coach says to the players on the bench.

Rashid and Tad stand up as well as the players waiting to bat. As soon as Tad stands up, Bradford springs into action. He unzips the bag a tiny bit more. He takes a deep breath. When he exhales, a stream of fire drills into Tad's water bottle. It works. A trickle of water flows out from the side. Bradford smiles and slips back into the bag to watch.

Niles is still at the plate. The count is two strikes, two balls. One more strike, and Niles will be out. Niles swings the bat at the perfect time. The crack of the bat tells Bradford and everyone in the bleachers that this ball is going far. The crowd cheers. Vinnie and Sammy run to home base. Niles runs to first base. He runs to second base. He runs to third base. A triple! Coach Fartzer jumps up and down. Otis hits a pop-up to the outfield. It is caught easily. Luke and Connor get on base, but Nick and Scotty strike out. The Clearview Dry Cleaners are winning 4-0.

"Hey! Who cut this hole in my water bottle?" yells Tad.

Uh-oh, thinks Niles. That sounds like something Bradford would do. But when he looks in his bag, there is no Bradford to be seen.

Then Niles sees Rashid eating a peanut butter sandwich at the end of the bench. *Oh no.*

How many kids don't put jelly on their sandwiches?

"Hey, Rashid. How are you doing?" asks Niles.

"I'm rweally gwood," he says as he chews his sandwich. He swallows. "That was a nice shot to the outfield." He pats Niles on the back with his sticky fingers.

"Thanks." As Niles talks, his eyes dart around looking for Bradford. He sees him out of the corner of his eye. Bradford sees Niles, too, and pulls his tiny hands back into Rashid's bag. "That's a nice bag you have there," says Niles.

"Thanks. It was my brother's bag. He said I could have it."

Niles puts his hand on the bag. He touches the pocket where he knows Bradford is hiding. "Do you have any gum or sunflower seeds?" Niles asks.

"Sure. Mom packed me lots of food. I sit on the bench, so I need to keep up my strength. Let me check."

"Oh no! That's okay," says Niles, waving away Rashid's hand. "You keep eating. I will check." Niles unzips the side pocket and grabs hold of Bradford by the tail. Bradford lets out a high-pitched scream.

"What was that?" asks Rashid.

"Maybe it was my stomach. I *am* pretty hungry." Niles grabs Bradford and a big bag of chips at the same time. He carries them both back to his bag. He drops Bradford inside his bag. *"Stay!"* he says.

"Huh?" asks Rashid.

"Boys, let's go! We are in the field," says Coach.

"Here, Rashid. Thanks for the chips. I guess I will have to eat later."

Niles runs back to second base. Tad holds his water bottle upside down. It is empty now. He throws it against the fence. Bradford smiles from inside Niles's bag.

Chapter 4:

Niles and Bradford have a long talk before the next baseball game.

"You cannot hide in my bat bag, Bradford. If you get caught, they will take you away from me. Remember when I found you in the woods after your last family threw you out when you were discovered?"

Bradford nods his head sadly like he understands. "But I like your games," he says.

"I promise to give you a play-by-play of the whole game," says Niles.

"Can I have extra peanut butter sandwiches?" Bradford puts his hands together and begs.

"Yes. I will bring you extra sandwiches. But, you stay put." Niles points to his dresser drawer. Bradford likes to sleep in Niles's socks, especially the red, fuzzy kind.

The game against the Fisher Fruit Market team is not going well for the Clearview Dry Cleaners. It is the first day team members are pitching. Kyle is super excited to pitch. It is the day he has been waiting for. He did not know the Fisher Fruit Market team would be so good, though. They are losing 5-2. Niles has struck out three times. *Sometimes that happens*, the Coach tells him. He still feels bad, though. Scotty trips over the ball on his way to first base. He is called out for that. Three outs. *Why? How come? What did I do wrong?* He has a lot of questions.

"Rashid," says Coach Fartzer. "Go in for Scotty. He and I need to chat."

"All right, Coach! Yes, Sir! I am on it. I am *on it!*" Rashid skips to right field.

Coach answers all of Scotty's questions while trying to coach the game at the same time. Niles drops a ball. He picks it up and tries to tag out the runner at second base, but he is too late. The runner is safe.

"Way to go, Loose Fingers!"

Coach does not hear Tad. He is too busy coaching. He has called a timeout.

But someone else hears Tad. Bradford pops out of Niles's batting helmet.

Before he gets caught, Bradford jumps onto the bench behind Tad. He is the only one in the dugout. He is supposed to be in the huddle during timeout, but he does not care. Bradford swipes the hat off Tad's head.

"Hey!" Tad jumps up and turns around, but Bradford has gone *poof* and is back in the batting helmet. Tad picks up his hat. He puts it on his head.

Coach and Scotty return to the dugout. They stand at the fence. This time Niles catches a pop-up fly ball. Two outs.

While the crowd is clapping, Bradford jumps out of the batting helmet. He stands behind Tad's feet. He steps over a pile of sunflower seeds that Tad is spitting out. He feels like it is raining. Bradford finishes his job just as the team runs back toward the dugout. He *poofs* back into the batting helmet.

"Tad, you're batting for Nick! Grab a helmet."

Tad stands up. He steps forward. At least he tries. He falls down and lands on the ground. His knee bleeds. "What? What?" he yells.

"Quit clowning around, Tad. Let's go."

"Coach, I...I can't."

"What do you mean?" Coach asks.

Tad points to his feet. His shoelaces are knotted together.

"Vinnie, get Tad a bandage. Sammy, untie those knots. *Who did this?*"

No one has ever heard anyone yell this loud. No one answers. Even Scotty doesn't ask a question. Rashid does not smile.

Bradford does not dare move from his hiding place. He starts to wonder if he went too far with his tricks.

Tad gets to bat. He hits a double and runs to second base, even with a banged-up knee. But it's not enough. The next time the Fisher Fruit Market is up to bat, their star player hits a homerun. They lead 12-2. The game is over.

But the night is not over for the Clearview Dry Cleaners. Coach makes them run—a lot. Around and around and around the bases. All because of Bradford. Niles knows. He always knows.

Chapter 5:

"I am sorry, Niles," says Bradford. "But that kid Tad is a big bully. He needed to be taught a lesson."

"That is not your job, Bradford," says Niles. He throws his uniform in the laundry basket. "I don't need to make enemies. I am new here. If Tad finds out my friend put a hole in his water bottle or knocked off his hat or tied his laces together, things will be worse for me. Plus, you are kind of being like a bully, too."

"I am sorry, Niles," says Bradford. He hangs his head. He turns his bottom lip upside down. It is hard for Niles to stay mad at him.

"Anyway," says Niles. "I have an idea to make things better. It might not work, but I need to try. You have to stay here this time."

"I will. I promise," says Bradford.

"You said that last time."

"No, I did not. I said I would not hide in your bat bag. I hid in your helmet. Plus, I did not promise. You know I never break my promises."

Niles sighs. "I know. Do not come with me today. There is a pool party at Rashid's house for the baseball team. Do not come. Do not hide in my swimming bag. Do not ride in my mom's car. Stay in my room—in the dresser. Okay? Promise," says Niles.

"I promise," says Bradford. They shake on it.

Chapter 6:

Rashid greets everyone on the team at his pool. He hasn't stopped smiling since the first boy arrived.

Most of the kids are splashing in the pool when Niles gets there. It is the first party he has been invited to since he moved to Clearview. He wants this party to go well.

Tad is jumping off the diving board. He is jumping high in the air and trying to make his splashes as big as he can. Niles remembers his plan. He jumps into the side of the pool and swims to the middle. Tad sees him. He quickly gets out of the pool and jumps off the diving board again. He jumps extra high so that he lands extra hard. Niles braces for impact. As soon as the waves hit, he is tossed around like a submarine from the game of Battleship in a huge ocean, but he's prepared.

"Good one, Tad," says Niles. "That was *awesome!*"

"Huh?" says Tad.

"Riding your waves! That was fun!" says Niles again.

"Yeah, do it again," says Scotty. "Wait, what is he doing?"

Everyone laughs, even Tad. For the next fifteen minutes, all of the kids from the baseball team wait in the middle of the pool for Tad to make waves with his gigantic jumps. It's a great time.

When Tad looks tired, Niles makes his move. "Want to play catch in the yard?" he asks.

"With you?" Tad looks down his nose at Niles.

"Yes," says Niles. "I want to get better before the county tournament on Saturday.

"You *could* use some practice."

Niles ignores the rude comment.

At first, Tad throws the baseball extra hard so that Niles has to chase it down every time. They don't have their baseball mitts. Then, when Niles doesn't give up, Tad throws the ball with better aim. They even try a game of seeing how many throws they can make before someone drops the ball. When Niles finally drops the ball at number thirty-one, he waits for Tad's mean comment.

Instead something else happens.

"Nice try, Niles. Your slippery fingers aren't so bad after all."

It is the closest thing to a compliment Niles has ever gotten from Tad.

Chapter 7:

Bradford is making smoke circles from his mouth the morning of the county baseball tournament. The circles are getting bigger and bigger and bigger.

"Bradford, stop it!" says Niles. "You are going to burn down my bedroom!"

"Oops, sorry! But did you *see* the size of those smoke circles?"

"Yes, good job. I need to focus. Today is a big day."

"I know. I know—big baseball day. I am excited, too!"

Niles looks down at Bradford. "Why are you excited?"

"Because I looooovvveeeee baseball!"

"Bradford, you are *not* going to the games,"
he says.

"Come on. I will be good."

"Niles! Time to go!" says Niles's dad from
downstairs.

"I have to go! Be good!"

Niles leaves the room before making
Bradford promise not to come to the games.
Bradford has all the time he needs to *poof* into the
bat bag as Niles rushes out the door.

Chapter 8:

The crowds go crazy when the kids take the field. The first game is between the Clearview Dry Cleaners and the Bakersville Sweet Shop. Kyle is pitching great. The bats are flying for the Clearview Dry Cleaners. Connor and Luke hit back-to-back homeruns. Even Scotty hits the ball. He makes it to first base. He does not have any questions about what he is supposed to do next. They win 9-3.

"Great job, boys! Bats on balls. Balls caught in the air. Balls scooped off the ground. Awesome throws. Great teamwork," says Coach Fartzer.

"Yee-haw!" comes a quiet voice from inside Niles's bag.

"Did you say something?" Rashid asks Niles.

Niles clears his throat. "Uh, no, I have a tickle in my throat." Niles kicks his bat bag to give a message. *Bradford.*

"Get some water, boys. We have fifteen minutes before the championship game."

Some of the boys leave to use the bathroom. Some go to get money from their parents to buy food at the concession stand. Niles unzips his bag. He looks inside. Bradford is hiding behind his extra baseballs at the bottom of the bag.

Niles whispers into the bag. "You are not supposed to be here."

Bradford whispers back, "You didn't make me promise."

Niles sighs.

"Don't be mad, Niles. You won! You won!" Bradford gets more excited.

"Shhhh!" he says.

"Did you say something?" asks Scotty.

"Sorry! I'm…uh…I'm just giving myself a pep talk for the next game," says Niles.

"Don't be nervous. You are doing great. Are you nervous? Are you scared?"

"No, Scotty. Thanks. I am good." Niles gets up to talk to his family before the next game. There is nothing more he can do with Bradford right now.

But before he leaves the dugout, Niles overhears one more conversation.

"Tad," says Coach Fartzer.

"Yes?" He pushes the big wad of gum in his mouth over to his cheek, so he can talk.

"Be ready to go in for the next game. I'm not sure if Otis is going to last the whole game. He's not feeling well. Your attitude's been better, too. Do you think you are ready—if I need you?"

"Yes, Coach Fart…yes, Coach. I'm ready." Tad sits up a little taller.

Niles hears Bradford from inside his bag. "Yee-haw!"

Niles clears his throat again. "Sorry, guys. I'm going to get some water now." Niles kicks his bag one more time before he leaves the dugout. At least his best friend can forgive Tad. If Tad is cool, Bradford's cool. And that is cool with Niles.

Chapter 9:

Rashid catches the first ball of the inning to make the first out of the game. Coach agrees to let him play one inning. He has a huge smile on his face. Bradford watches from inside Niles's helmet which is hanging on the fence. He jumps up and down. Niles gives Rashid a thumbs up.

The Southside Butchers are much tougher than the Clearview Dry Cleaners. Even their name sounds harsh. Their next three batters crank the ball to the outfield in the gaps on the field between the outfield players. Even though Scotty knows how to move now, it's impossible to get to those balls in time. Vinnie makes a leaping dive for one of the hardest hit balls, but it slips past his glove.

After the first inning, the score is 3-0. The Clearview Dry Cleaners are losing.

"Boys, don't give up. We have been down before," says Coach. "Stay loose. Stay alert. Watch the ball. And have some fun. You look nervous out there."

Hands in the middle, and the boys yell, *"Team!"*

There are four scoreless innings after that. Kyle is pitching well, but they are still losing 3-0. Bradford is getting bored. He lifts his nose in the air and sniffs. *Sunflower seeds, grape bubble gum, beef jerky (gross!), peanut bu…peanut butter!*

He jumps out of the batting helmet without looking. Rashid almost steps on him. Bradford *poofs* to the bag that smells like peanut butter. It's Coach Fartzer's bag. He didn't have time to finish his lunch between games. Bradford grabs the sandwich. He rips off the crust. He throws it out of the bag. The sandwich is gone before the Clearview Dry Cleaners get back to the dugout. They are batting next.

"Last at bat boys. If we don't score at least three runs, the game is over. I am proud of your hard work. It is time to show this team what we have inside. Dig deep. Let's put some bats to some balls!"

The first batter up this inning is Scotty. He's the last batter in the line-up. Then the batting order starts over with Connor. Scotty looks scared.

He looks at Coach like he has a ton of questions to ask like, *Do I have to bat? Are you sure about this? What if I strike out?* But Coach just pats him on the shoulder as he runs past him to coach the team from third base.

Scotty does not swing at the first two pitches. That is a good thing. The first pitch was high—a ball. The second pitch was low—a ball. The next two pitches, Scotty does not swing, either. That was a bad thing. They were strikes. With two strikes, everyone waits to see what he will do next.

"Swing the bat. Swing the bat." Tad is talking to himself. A lot of people are thinking the same thing. At least he isn't screaming at Scotty.

Scotty puts the bat on his shoulder. The pitch flies toward him. It is low. He does not swing. The crowd lets out their breath at the same time. The pitch count is three balls, two strikes, one more pitch to go.

Scotty looks like he is shaking. He watches Coach. He watches the pitcher. He closes his eyes. The pitcher lets loose.

"*Ball 4!* Batter take your base!" says the umpire.

The crowd cheers. Scotty runs to first base.

Connor and Luke hit singles. The bases are loaded. Otis bats next. There are no outs. Otis does not look well. He walks to home plate. He sways from side to side. He uses his bat to hold himself upright. Then Otis throws up on home plate. The crowd gasps.

"Tad!" yells Coach Fartzer. "You are going in for Otis!"

Tad stands up quickly. He steps on Coach's bag and uses the fence to stop himself from falling. He knocks Niles's helmet off the fence.

"Eek!" says Bradford. He pops out of the bag. His fists are ready to attack. Then he remembers where he is and *poofs* back to Niles's bag before he is spotted.

"Yes, Coach. I can do it."

After home plate is cleaned off, Tad walks to the plate. He takes a deep breath, looks at Coach, and lifts his bat. He takes the first pitch with his bat, sending the ball into the gap between left field and center field.

"Scotty, run!" yells Coach.

The crowd for the Clearview Dry Cleaners goes wild. Niles sees Nora and his mom and dad jumping up and down.

Scotty and Connor score runs. The team is down 2 runs to 3. The Southside Butchers are winning. Tad stands on second base and Luke on third base. Nick bats next. He pops up to third base. The third baseman catches the ball. Out number one.

Vinnie bats next. He fouls the first three pitches. Then the pitcher throws a ball so fast that Vinnie swings and misses. Out two.

Niles grabs his helmet. Bradford's hand pops out. He gives Niles a high-five before *poofing* back to his bag. Two outs, down by one run. Niles can hear Nora and his parents cheering from the crowd.

"Do your best, Niles. You are ready," says Coach.

"Let's go, Niles. You can do it!" yells Tad from second base.

Niles makes the walk to home plate. It seems like a long way to go. He puts the bat on his shoulder and gets into position. The first pitch is a ball. The pitch is high. Niles does not swing. The second ball looks good to Niles. He swings and fouls the ball. Strike one. Two more balls follow.

Niles knows he must have a hit to keep the game alive. Three balls, one strike.

"Come on, Niles!"

"Hit the ball!"

"Let's go, Clearview!"

The crowd is electric.

Rashid is pacing the dugout back and forth. His smile has been replaced by a bad case of nervous stomach that makes him frown.

Niles steps away from the base. He takes another deep breath.

Bradford watches from the opening in Niles's bat bag. He thinks about blowing fire at the pitcher but decides that would be a bad idea. He holds his breath instead.

Niles stares at the pitcher. The ball leaves the pitcher's glove. His bat makes contact with the ball.

"Foul!" yells the umpire.

Three balls, two strikes, full count. If he strikes out, the game is over.

"Niles! Niles! Niles! Niles!" The crowd is chanting his name.

Coach Fartzer nods his head at Niles to keep his hopes up. Niles pulls the bat back to his shoulder. The ball flies at him from the pitcher. It's a good pitch. He swings the bat with all his might. He doesn't have time to watch the ball. He runs and runs and runs. When he makes it to second base, his teammates storm the field. Luke scores.

Tad scores the winning run. The Clearview Dry Cleaners win the county championship 4-3.

"I am so proud of you boys," says Coach. "You came together. Everyone was important. Whether you sat on the bench or filled in for a sick player or started the game, you were all important. You finally understood what it means to be a team."

"Party at my house!" yells Rashid.

Niles can't stop smiling. Now he knows how Rashid feels. It feels good.

"Niles."

Niles slings his bag over his shoulder and turns around. Tad is standing there. "Yes?"

"I am sorry," says Tad. He kicks a rock in the dugout.

"About what?" asks Niles.

"I was a jerk when the season started. I blamed you for taking my second base spot. I think the Coach didn't like my attitude, either. Anyway, you are not so bad after all."

"Thanks, Tad," says Niles.

"But…uh…don't tell anyone about this. I don't…uh…I don't want anyone thinking I'm turning soft."

"Sure, Tad. No problem."

Niles walks toward the car where his family is waiting. Bradford keeps running around in his bag. He can't sit still. He is so excited.

"Bradford, *chill!*" says Niles.

"I can't. I am happy, happy, *happy!*"

Niles laughs. "Me, too. But you need to settle down."

"How? How? How?" Bradford giggles as he rolls around in the bag.

"I will give you extra peanut butter sandwiches for dinner."

Bradford sits perfectly still. He will do anything for the promise of peanut butter sandwiches. If only that would solve all of life's problems.

Please consider leaving a review on Amazon.

Thank you.

Other Children's Books by Marcy Blesy:

Niles and Bradford, Baseball Bully

There are two things that nine-year-old Niles can count on when his family moves to a new town. One, his love for trying new sports will help him meet people. Two, his friendship with his pet dragon Bradford means he will never be alone. However, when a bully on the baseball team makes life hard for Niles, Bradford's idea of helping his friend gets him banned from the game.

Niles and Bradford, Basketball Shots

There are two things that nine-year-old Niles can count on when his family moves to a new town. A sport loving boy and his pet dragon. One, his love for trying new sports will help him meet people. Two, his friendship with his pet dragon Bradford means he will never be alone. However, when things do not go as well as planned during an important basketball game, Niles starts to doubt himself.

Niles and Bradford, Soccer Kicks

There are two things that nine-year-old Niles can count on when his family moves to a new town. One, his love for trying new sports will help him meet people. Two, his friendship with his pet dragon Bradford means he will never be alone. However, when a show-off soccer player steals the attention of Bradford, things go downhill for Niles.

Niles and Bradford, Track Team

There are two things that nine-year-old Niles can count on when his family moves to a new town. One, his love for trying new sports will help him meet people. Two, his friendship with his pet dragon Bradford means he will never be alone. However, an unexpected track injury and an unexpected new friend teach him the real meaning of a team.

Evie and the Volunteers Series

Join ten-year-old Evie and her friends as they volunteer all over town meeting lots of cool people and getting into just a little bit of trouble. There is no place left untouched by their presence, and what they get from the people they meet is greater than any amount of money.

Book 1   *Animal Shelter*

Book 2   *Nursing Home*

Book 3   *After-School Program*

Book 4   *Food Pantry*

Book 5:   *Public Library*

Book 6:   *Hospital*

Book 7   *Military Care Packages*

Dax and the Destroyers: (a new *Evie and the Volunteers* spin-off featuring a popular character)

Book 1:   House Flip

Twelve-year-old Dax spends the summer with his Grandma. When a new family moves into the run-down house across the street, Dax finds a fast friend in their son Harrison. Not to be outdone by his friends, Evie and the Volunteers, and all of their good deeds, Dax finds himself immersed in the business of house flipping as well as Harrison's family drama. But don't expect things to go smoothly when Evie and her friends get word of this new volunteer project. Everyone has an opinion about flipping this house.

Book 2:   Park Restoration

Am I Like My Daddy?

Join seven-year-old Grace on her journey through coping with the loss of her father while learning about the different ways that people grieve the loss of a loved one. In the process of learning about who her father was through the eyes of others, she learns about who she is today because of her father's personality and love. *Am I Like My Daddy?* is a book designed to help children who are coping with the loss of a loved one. Children are encouraged to express through journaling what may be so difficult to express through everyday conversation. *Am I Like My Daddy?* teaches about loss through reflection.

Am I Like My Daddy? is an important book in the children's grief genre. Many books in this genre deal with the time immediately after a loved one dies. This book focuses on years after the death, when a maturing child is reprocessing his or her grief. New questions arise in the child's need to fill in those memory gaps.

Be the Vet:

Do you like dogs and cats?

Have you ever thought about being a veterinarian?

Place yourself as the narrator in seven unique stories about dogs and cats. When a medical emergency or illness impacts the pet, you will have the opportunity to diagnose the problem and suggest treatment. Following each story is the treatment plan offered by Dr. Ed Blesy, a 20 year practicing veterinarian. You will learn veterinary terms and diagnoses while being entertained with fun, interesting stories.

This is the first book in the BE THE VET series.

For ages 9-12

Be the Vet, Volume 2

Made in the USA
Monee, IL
15 December 2020